To Audrey, who loves horses—
and to Dolly, Freckles, Honey, and Blue, the horses we loved.

E
401-1238

A FEIWEL AND FRIENDS BOOK
An Imprint of Macmillan

THE LOST AND FOUND PONY. Copyright © 2011 by Tracy Dockray.
All rights reserved. Printed in April 2011 in China by Macmillan Production (Asia) Ltd., Kwun Tong,
Kowloon, Hong Kong. Supplier Code: 10. For information, address Feiwel and Friends,
175 Fifth Avenue, New York, N.Y. 10010.

Library of Congress Cataloging-in-Publication Data available

ISBN: 978-0-312-59259-2

Book design by Elizabeth Tardiff

Feiwel and Friends logo designed by Filomena Tuosto

First Edition: 2011

10 9 8 7 6 5 4 3 2 1

mackids.com

The Lost and Found Pony

Tracy Dockray

FEIWEL AND FRIENDS
New York

I didn't ask to be so small.

When I was born, my mother towered over me.

I couldn't wait to grow up.

And when I did, I realized we were *both* small. But we could still run fast, fast enough that the wind would tickle our manes.

And even though we couldn't carry much, I knew
that I would be just right for someone small like me.

One day, I was washed and brushed, and dressed up with a bow.
I was going to be a girl's wish come true. When she saw me, the girl
threw her arms around me and whispered that I was perfect. And I
felt perfect. Nothing could be better than that day.

Over time, I learned to jump with the girl upon my back.
We loved jumping and won many competitions. With each
blue ribbon, the girl's parents became more proud.

Until one day, I came to a jump that was just too high. Everyone gasped as the girl tumbled into the dust. When she got up, she took my reins and told me that it wasn't my fault.

"That animal could have gotten you *killed!*" her mother shrieked. "This is terrible—how can you possibly win on a pony like this?"

The girl's worried
parents led her away.

I didn't see the girl for two weeks. I waited for my friend
day after day, wondering what I had done wrong.

Then I found out. The problem wasn't what I had done, but what I *was*. The girl wasn't allowed to ride me anymore because I was too small for her now. She had been given a big horse with a smooth, shiny coat that could run faster and jump higher than a tiny, little pony.

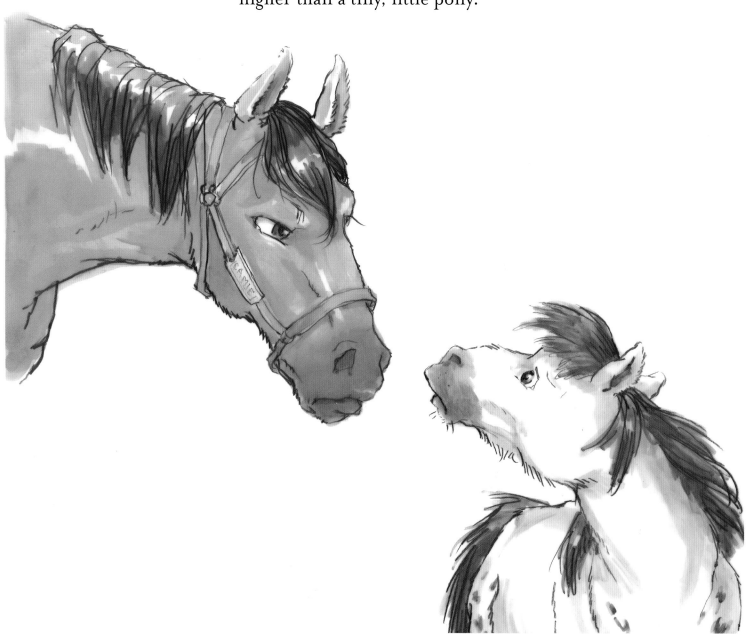

That evening, the girl came into my stall. I was so happy she came back. I remember her hugging my neck and saying, "Even though I can't ride you, I will never let you go. I will always love you."

But how can a little girl change things? The next day, when the girl wasn't home, a man came and took me away. I was sad and scared to leave my home.

After a long, dusty day on the road, we drove up to an enormous tent.

I was unloaded and brought to an old trailer. A tiny man appeared, even smaller than the girl. He was to be my new owner. I was to be a circus pony.

We were a team and everyone loved us. In the circus, being small was what made us special. Each night after the show, the man would feed and groom me, all the while talking of our day in a soft voice.

The circus moved from town to town and we now starred in the center ring. Yet even as the crowds cheered us, I always looked to the stands, hoping the little girl might be in them.

While we were the heroes of the circus, the years passed quickly. But eventually, I grew too old to jump through flaming hoops, though I could do many things the people still clapped for. And all the while, I never gave up my search.

At first, we hardly noticed the applause getting quieter as the crowds thinned. Then slowly, it happened. The big top that held our circus seemed too big with its stands so empty. Over the years, our audience had developed different tastes. They stayed home now, playing video games or watching movies for spectacle and fun.

But what would become of us?

The answer came soon enough. Our circus was to be sold off in bits and pieces.

The elephants and exotic animals were sold to zoos all over.

What would happen to me? The man came to whisper good-bye, for I belonged to the circus and could not go away with him. At that moment, my heart felt too big for my small chest and I thought it might break.

All the circus horses were carted off to be sold at auction. The horses there were like me, hobbly old things that had been around. Most of them were sold and carried off in large trucks. No one noticed me for some time, but when it was finally my turn to be sold, I tried not to be scared. I remembered my life as a show jumper and famous circus performer. I held up my head and tried to look as proud as a tiny, very old pony could.

And then someone bought me.

I didn't know what would happen to me, but I knew that
my heart could not stand being outgrown again. I saw a
lady striding through the crowd.

As she came closer and smiled, I realized it was the little girl! All these years, I'd been searching the stands for her, but of course, little girls grow up.

"Hello, my old friend. I knew that was you. Where have you *been*?" I couldn't answer. But she hugged me and explained that after I was sold, she gave up competing, but never her love of horses.

She now runs a stable. I will help the children who need extra care since I am small, slow, and gentle.

And here, I know I'll never be outgrown again.
I will always have children who love to ride me and
pretend that I am their own dream come true.

Author's Note

Several years ago in Texas, I encountered a very old party pony. As I led my young daughter around on his swayed back, I wondered where he had started and what had happened in his long life. When it was time to stop, my daughter wouldn't let go of the saddle. She was too young to understand that this was her pony only for that short ride. As we drove away, I thought that Black Beauty told his story, and now it was time that this very old pony got to tell his.

The pony I met was lucky that he was so loved at the tail end of his life. But many horses are considered useless when they are no longer strong and fast. They are auctioned off to people and places where they are not loved. In this book, the pony asks, "But how can a little girl change things?" You will be happy to know that *you* can help change things. There are organizations that rescue horses from auction houses and place them in loving homes for the rest of their lives. One near me is Amaryllis Farm Equine Rescue and Sanctuary (www.forrascal.com). Do horses have dreams? I believe that they do, and we will help them come true.